Introduction

GW00786573

My name is Bobtor, I was once very bored sat in a sh
to choose me to come home with them. One day a m
straight away he needed me. He looked like he had a
went home with him and he told my very important job was to look after his
friend Lou who was moving away from the Isle of Wight to the mainland all
by herself. His name was Big Rob.

Turns out I have the best job in the world as for years Lou and I have
travelled and gone on amazing adventures and I am so lucky to have her as
my owner. My little brother William (who is bigger than me!) Came along
and we became inseparable. He is so cheeky if not a bit lazy and a bit of a
piggy when it comes to snackies!

Our friends loved our photos and stories of our days out so much we set up
our Bearygoodfun facebook page and they encouraged me to try writing a
book!

We started cycling during the Covid-19 lockdown on our trusty bike Bobby.
We managed to cycle 1084 miles which is the distance from Lands End to
John O'Groats. We did it all virtually as during lockdown you aren't allowed
to go outside but we still got a lovely shiny medal too.

Because we love cycling and the Isle of Wight so much, we decided we
needed a proper adventure and when the lockdown restrictions were lifted
and we were allowed we planned our trip and I wanted to share our story
with you.

MONDAY 6TH JULY 2020

And so begins our epic adventure. An early start but we made it down to the ferry in good time all the way from home. William had his new crash helmet on and I was safely in my seat belt. Bobby Bike raced along even though he was laden down with all our buckets and spades and William had stuffed biscuits in any gaps when Lou wasn't looking. Typical William! We had our packed lunch too.

The weather was lovely but not too hot. We have just got on the car ferry from Southampton docks. The ferry is called Red Funnel. Bobby Bike is safely parked and we are enjoying a little rest. It's such a big boat. We have managed to get a seat by the window and a great view. You have to wear a mask on the ferry now as there is the nasty virus.

William has realised you can't eat snacks through a mask! We want to go out on the outside deck later for a better look and fresh air. You are allowed to take your mask off outside so William will finally get a biscuit! He is having withdrawal! I am so excited about seeing our tent house and later tonight Nanny is coming to tea.

We have been on 2 ferries now! We went on the great big car ferry and now a little tiny chain ferry to take us from East Cowes to Cowes. We were only on the little one a matter of minutes but it's really rattily, even more than Bobby Bike. Lou explained that it is actually pulled across by a great big chain. It is called a floating bridge.

We cycled Bobby Bike all the way along the lovely quiet and flat cycle path through to Sandown. It was a lovely ride and called the Red Squirrel trail. Red Squirrels live on the isle of Wight but not at home. They have to be looked after as they are rare now and special. We didn't see any as we cycled but Lou said it was probably and Bobby Bike is so noisy and Williams singing may have scared them away. Shame as William was singing his own little song about squirrels!

Our cycle path gave us glimpse of a river called the medina and along a lovely tree lined shady path into Newport. That is the centre if the island with lots of shops and where our Nanny and Grandad work. From Newport we followed the path along the river and through the trees towards Sandown. We passed fields and loads of beautiful wild flowers and lovely scenery of lush green hills. Williams head was whipping round so fast as he was trying to take it in and make sure he saw everything!

When we got to Sandown we popped out and went along the road to our campsite in Shanklin. We cycled past our Nanny's house and William was waving and dinging the bell frantically until Lou reminded him Nanny was at work! He wasn't too bothered as he had still got to ding the bell which he does love!

We have just got to our tent in Lower Hyde Shanklin. It is perfect. William and I have our own bedroom with proper beds. The first thing William and I did whilst Lou was trying to sort Bobby Bike was run in and choose our beds. I was faster at running than William so I got first pick and chucked my rucksack on the left bed and had a bounce to check it was a good bed. I've not slept in a tent before but William has when he goes night time fishing with Ivan. Lou says we aren't camping but glamping! The tent is so big Bobby Bike fits inside. There is a kitchen and everything! It's a bit flappy when the wind blows which makes William a bit nervous but I've reminded him that we are brave adventurers. We have already run around and been in all the cupboards and drawers so it must be time for a spot of lunch.

Whilst Lou was unpacking William and I went to explore the campsite with the park map. We saw the toilet block which was well fancy and modern and we saw where the hand sanitising point was so we could make sure our paws were clean. On our adventure round the park we saw a play park with swings and a climbing frame. William wanted to play on it but his little paws couldn't reach high enough no matter how high he jumped. On reflection it probably would have been too much like exercise for William if he had made it up there so it was probably a blessing in disguise! Even thinking about it made him need to sit down and have a custard cream! We also saw a sports court for ball games that some bigger boys were playing at and a swimming pool. The pool had a curly slide! We don't like getting our fur wet so we hurried past and saw that there was an amusement arcade and shop and also a restaurant. Williams tummy growled at the sniffy wiff of chips coming from the restaurant so we popped into the little shop and used some of our holiday spends Ivan gave us for sticks of rock. William didn't moan walking back to the tent as we were both happily slurping our sticks of rock. William stuck his tongue out and it was all rainbow colours from the rock. Mind you so were his mooshes where he had dribbled and got sticky from the rock all round his mouth!

It was lovely having nanny over for tea at the tent. She was so excited and we showed her round whilst Lou made paella for tea. We haven't seen her for months and months because of the yucky virus making people poorly. We have sat out on the decking until way past our bed time chatting to nanny and telling her about our Bobby Bike adventures over lockdown and how we got a shiny medal doing it. We even had a slice of cheesecake which was amazing. As always William got it all over his mooshes. Its been an amazing first day to our holiday. Nanny is sleeping in the tent too. William was so excited we thought he would never fall asleep but after a while we realised he had gone quiet and found him curled up asleep on the bed, luckily his not mine!

Nanny stayed the night in our tent. We had breakfast outside the tent with Nanny. Scrambled eggs. Very yummy. It was lovely sitting at our fancy table and chairs on the decking, saying good morning to everybody. After we picked scrambled egg out of William's fur, we went to our Great Nannys house. We took our shiny medal to show her. She even put it on and tried to make out she won it! We weren't allowed to cuddle Great Nanny because of social distancing and we don't want her to get poorly. This is also the reason he thinks William didn't get his usual biscuit or 10 as she couldn't get close enough to hear his rumbly tummy! William is normally full of cake and biscuits by the time he waddles out of Great Nannys!

We have just back from a Bobby Bike adventure to the Garlic Farm at Newchurch. The weather was lovely and sunny so we cruised along the cycle path following Williams super sniffy hooter all the way. We bought all our favourites in the Garlic Farm shop including Williams favourite Bbq Sauce with garlic and my favourite garlic mayonnaise. We bought lots of new things to try too. We loved it in the shop.

There was actual garlic in there too. I think its one of my favourite places ever! We even went for a nice walk around some wild flowers looking for bees and learning about all the different types of garlic. Turns out there is more than just "stinky" and "very stinky" like William says!

We have just cycled back from the Garlic Farm and went the special way along the seafront from Sandown to Shanklin. The tide was right in and we could barely see any sand at all. We saw lots of pretty coloured beach huts though. There were some people playing in the sea. We managed to get past all the ice cream cafes with William trying to escape by giving him a bag of garlic farm pork scratchings to suck on all the way home.

Even William knows you can't eat more when you are already eating! The big hill back up from the beach was very hard work as it was windy and Bobby Bike was weighed down with all our garlicky shopping. William was extra stinky after having all that garlic!

Auntie came for tea tonight. It was lovely to see her. She liked our tent lots and we had bolognaise for dinner. William ate mainly cheese though! Auntie didn't stay as she says she has to go to work tomorrow but I think like me, she is worried about Williams garlicky botty coughs stinking out the tent!

William was quite tired and worn out from all our adventures and also really hates walking so he decided to rest today and munch through some snacks from the Garlic Farm. (I remembered to leave a window open!) I was still full of beans so I went out for a walk with Lou and Grandad. We started by going along the dis used railway line by our campsite. The trains used to go along here all the way to Ventnor. We walked up over Shanklin Down and towards Luccombe Down. It was so misty and it looked like we could be in a scary film.

It was so misty we accidently managed to walk round in a big circle and eventually the mist cleared and we could see really far. We even saw Grandad's house from up high. We sat down for a yum picnic on Luccombe down. William was upset that he missed out on picnic when I got home and told him. Refreshed and refuelled we carried on and walked down through a place called "Devil's Chimney". It is steep steps down through a narrow tunnel of rocks and it is a bit creepy. It's at a place called the Landslip and its where some of the ground had fallen down into the sea.

We came back through Luccombe and stopped for a cup of tea on the cliff before walking back along the seafront. It was 10 miles we worked out that we had walked. Lou and I are so tired we have decided to have a quiet night in the tent with William. We snuggled down with left over bolognaise from yesterday, William polishing off the cheese and whilst Lou read her book, we watched a film on her phone.

THURSDAY 9TH JULY 2020

It's another wet and misty day but we don't let that stop us. We put on our macs and hopped on Bobby Bike. We followed the lovely cycle path through to Wroxall and Lou showed us the house she was born in. The route took us past Appledurcombe House which was a very grand house but all the mist made it tricky to see.

Lou cycled up a big hill extra to try and get us nearer to see better but still no luck. That hill was great in the way back down though! Our ride turned into a real adventure when we had to ride Bobby Bike through a wet, grassy slippery field of sheep!! There were hundreds of them. They kept running in front of Bobby Bike. William has never seen a sheep up close before so he wandered over and tried to make friends with one by telling it all about his favourite snacks! He waddled up really close in his flowery mac but the sheep didn't mind. They probably see lots of badgers, I guess!

After battling through all the wildlife we passed through a fancy gate called Freemantle gate and had to go down a path that was really eroded and full of giant boulders. It was really scary and felt like Bobby Bike would shake apart. We had to hold on for dear life but being brave adventurers, we didn't cry but I could feel William shaking. We were so grateful to find a lovely smooth cycle path to take us back to the tent. Lou peddled fast as by now we were quite wet from the misty rain and a little distressed from the nasty path and Bobby Bike had a new rattle. We had to give William crumpets and jam to steady his nerves whilst Lou went out with Grandad. Big Rob is coming to see us tonight.

Yay Big Rob came. We haven't seen him in ages. He had already had his tea but we showed him round our tent and he really liked it. Him and Lou went out for a walk as we still need to socially distance a bit from Big Rob as if he got poorly it could make him really, really ill. I was so happy to see him though. I've missed him so much. I've sent him lots of letters and cards over lockdown so that he knew I was thinking of him.

Its sunny again. Yay! We had a huge ride on Bobby Bike this morning. We headed down the seafront and had a little play on the sand. We met a man out running with his little boy who had a biscuit. We had to watch William though as we already could see the drool forming. The man was asking all about our adventure as he rides bikes too. He couldn't believe it when Lou said we had cycled the distance of the country in Bobby Bike. He thinks William us the first badger ever to do that! I am proud of William too although William found a giant ice cream and was licking it until he realised it was a plastic sign for the cafe! Silly William!

After we removed William from the plastic ice cream we carried on riding Bobby Bike along the red squirrel cycle path to Newport. From Newport we went on a new route that took us all the way to Ryde. We went past Quarr Abbey but didn't go and see the piggies as there was so many people there and Lou is still trying hard to keep us safe from the yukky virus. Quarr Abbey is where all the monks live. William got confused thinking Lou said Monkeys!! The monks keep piggies and you are allowed to buy pig food and feed them. There is also a cafe there that does amazing cakes but we steered William away from there or we would never get on! We decided to ride the road way back as it is quicker and William was getting hangry for his lunch! Ivan is coming to see us tonight and we are allowed fish and chips!

Hooray Ivan has arrived! Its so nice to see him. We all walked down to the seafront, yes even William walked and got a great big portion of fish, chips and mushy peas. We sat on the sea wall and ate them. There was lots of seagulls watching but the weren't brave enough or silly enough to try and take food from William! William and I shovelled our food in with William keeping one eye on the seagulls at all time being careful not to drop the tiniest crumb as we knew they would swoop down on us and pinch them all. We had a little walk along the sand and look at the sea. We even got an ice lolly for pudding. William loves it when Ivan's around! It was back to the tent as it was dark and past bedtime again. We are such dirty stop outs on holiday!

SATURDAY 11TH JULY 2020

We went to the beach AND had an ice cream. Lou cooked us all a full breakfast at the tent. William loves sausages! We went down the beach as it was lovely and sunny so we had our shades on and looked like proper cool dudes. I put on my new Hawaiian shirt and we laid out our towels on the sand.

I planned ahead and brought my own deckchair. We had a proper whippy ice cream with a flake and managed to eat it before it melted everywhere. William obviously got ice cream and flake chocolate all over his mooshes. We did a fantastic job of building sand castles too. Like a little village. We even put little sand castles on top of bigger ones. I'm so glad we brought our buckets and spades down with us. We did wander down to the water but it was too cold and wet for our liking!

This afternoon we rode the bus through Ventnor to Godshill. William loves riding the bus. He gets so excited to ring the bell. Lou had to make sure to sanitise his paws afterwards though because of the dangerous germs still around. When we got off at Godshill we walked up to the church and saw all the lovely thatched cottages. That is what Godshill is famous for. It was so pretty.

We then sat in a lovely tea garden and had a cream tea. It was delicious and fancy until William got jam and cream everywhere even up his nose! Auntie is coming to have a party at the tent tonight.

We had the biggest burgers for tea and chips with all sorts of yummy sauces and cheesey on it. It was all massive and so delicious and William went mad for the cheese. Auntie was a bit quiet as she was tired because she had too much wobbly pops the night before. It was so nice sitting outside the tent and we got to stay up past bed time again.

Auntie camped in our tent last night so it was exciting to see her when we woke up. Today we went on a nice walk along the cliff to Lake with Ivan and back along the beach.

Even William came with us but I think its because he overheard Lou suggesting an ice lolly to Ivan. From the cliff we could see down to the beach below and the lovely blue sea. We have to be very careful at the cliff edge as you could slip and fall. We went down to look at the water's edge again and we sat in some comfy deckchairs and had a yummy fruity lolly at Hinks beach cafe. The weather was beautiful and it was a lovely relaxing day.

We are going to have a quiet night at the tent to plan our next few days of adventure. We are sad that Ivan has had to go home now. Lou had promised us a big Bobby Bike ride tomorrow and even a pack lunch to take with us. William is so excited I wonder if he will even sleep tonight!

MONDAY 13TH JULY 2020

A lovely sunny day today and not too hot, perfect for a day on Bobby Bike. We left our tent nice and early and cycled our usual route through to Alverstone but then we went off on an epic adventure through Brading to Bembridge. There were some really big hills but when we got to Bembridge Lou tried to take us to the Windmill but sadly it was shut because of yukky virus. William has never seen a windmill. I have, I even went inside one when Lou and I went with Big Rob to Amsterdam. We went down to the lifeboat station as well. We stopped for a look but the lifeboat station and RNLI shop was closed too. We did see lots of people playing on the beach. It was really bright and the sea was so shimmery.

As we were leaving Bembridge we stopped at the Tollgate Cafe. Lou used to go there with her nan and grandad when she was a little girl. Lou had a nice coffee to give her the energy to carry on towards St. Helens. Luckily because we sat outside William hadn't noticed that they do cake and ice cream! Its always a drama when he tries to eat on Bobby Bike! On the way to St. Helens we saw all the houseboats. If I lived on a houseboat I would wear my captains hat everyday. William said he would wear his pirate hat.

After St.Helens we cycled through Nettlestone and Firestone Copse and eventually ended up at Wootton where we joined the cycle track that took us to Newport. We found a lovely spot for our picnic lunch over looking the River Medina and we sat on a giant tree stump. William was trying to look in the river for fishes! After lunch we had a fast ride back as our Nanny is coming round later and Lou has promised we can toast marshmoobles!

Nanny came for dinner and tried gnocchi for the first time. She liked them even though they look a bit like pale woodlice!!
We toasted marshmoobles with Nanny. She has never done it before so we showed her how. You have to be careful as the stick is pointy and the fire is super hot but she learnt quickly. William gets such sticky mooshes when marshmoobling! We have stayed up till well past our bedtime.

We had a fancy breakfast with Nanny of scrambled egg and bacon on toast. Nanny had jobs to do so we went out for a Bobby Bike ride. It was hot and cloudy and kept trying to rain. Lou called it "muggy" We thought it was a funny word!

We rode to East Cowes as the little chain ferry is broken so we have to ride a different way back in Friday and Lou wanted to see what it was like before we took Bobby Bike all laden down. We could do our normal route we like on the Red Squirrel train through to Newport and then along the medina on the greenway through all the trees but there was a big scary hilly road. It was a really steep hill and the cars were super-fast but it was only for a short while until we could get on to a quieter road but Lou says if we allow enough time and pack Bobby Bike well and all behave and be sensible, we will be ok. We were up so late last night with Nanny now we are very tired and looking forward to chilling out tonight whilst Lou goes to see her friend Emily. She has made us dinner and sorted Williams snacks for later. To be honest I am so tired I think I'll probably be fast asleep. William is already going all noddy as he eats his dinner!

WEDNESDAY 15TH JULY 2020

Today was a special day as William actually joined us for a walk. We went down the road from our tent and Lou took us through Sandown Airport. It wasn't like the airports we went to when we went to Venice or Jersey and the planes were teeny tiny. We were so lucky as we got to see a plane come in to land. We then got to see another one take off. They look like super fun planes. We know a man called Mike that can actually fly a plane and his friend was at Sandown airport. We wave at every plane in case it is Mike! We weren't allowed to get too close as its dangerous. We loved watching the planes. Auntie has flown a plane before. William would really love to try it but I worry his paws wouldn't reach the controls!

There was even a space rocket at the airport. A small one. We didn't see that take off! We were amazed by the rocket.

We carried on walking and went to Borthwood Copse. We had so much fun running around and playing hide and seek. We were climbing all over the tree stumps. As we walked back we had to go in a supermarket as Big Rob is coming for tea. Whilst Lou and I were looking for nice things William trailed behind flagging, tired from the walk, after a while we noticed the shuffling behind us had gone quiet and William had disappeared! We didn't panic as William is a simple creature. We headed to deli counter and found him with his snout pressed against the glass drooling over the cheesey. Lou apologised profusely to the nice lady and we dragged William away leaving a trail of badger snot on the counters glass screen! So embarrassing!

THURSDAY 16TH JULY 2020

Poor William and his selective hearing. All he heard was "car" and "picnic" this morning so merrily bundled into Grandad's car when he arrived. William didn't hear the word "walk" until we had driven out to Freshwater. Too exhausted from walking yesterday William decided he would wait in the car not realising that the picnic was for out on the walk.

We walked up great big hills and Grandad got covered in really big beetles. He named them Paul and Ringo. They wouldn't leave him alone. Eventually we made it to the Tennyson monument. It was massive. We weren't done yet, we carried on walking and we found a lovely spot for a picnic on West down. We had a lovely lunch and it was a nice spot to stop and have a rest. We could see so far and the views were beautiful. After a while we could see the needles lighthouse. Lou said there is a big walk for Charity where people walk from one side of the island to the other and the last bit is climbing up this great big hill at the end! That seems a bit mean finishing all that way up a great big hill. They do it in a day but I think it would take me a week and William a year!!! Auntie and Step Grandad have done it several times before and the sponsor pennies go towards the hospice.

We decided that it was sad that William missed out so when we got back to the car we would drive to Alum bay and get him an ice cream. William was dead chuffed with his rum and raisin cone and perked right up so we went for a little look in Yarmouth and a cold drink as we walked down the pier at Yarmouth pier. We are sad as tonight is our last night and we have to pack Bobby Bike tonight but we do get to see Nanny and Great Nanny tomorrow.

We are so sad. We went to see Nanny and Great Nanny this morning and as we are going home today Great Nanny didn't mind that William had found her biscuit stash and comfort munched his way through. I'm glad as he had been eyeing up our packed lunch for the journey already. We had tea at Great Nanny's house (and biscuits-says William) before we said our good byes and hoped on Bobby Bike.

The weather was gorgeous and we cycled along poor Bobby Bike creaking along under the weight of all our souvenirs and snacks. It was hard going up the big hill on the scary road at East Cowes but we didn't get off once and we made it to the ferry in loads of time.

We are now sat on the ferry with our masks on looking out the window at all the little boats. The big ferry had to honk his horn to tell a little boat to get out the way. It made William jump and we both fell about laughing as it scared a botty cough out of William that sounded a bit like the ferry horn.

Once we got off the ferry it was strange being back in busy Southampton but we cycled home to find Ivan waiting for us. He had missed us so much and we will sit in the garden with him having juice and a biscuit and telling him all about our adventures.

We have loved our holiday so much and can't wait for our next one.

Hopefully next time the yukky virus will have gone so we can see even more.

Printed in Great Britain
by Amazon

46145599R00017